DISNEP

CORY IN THE HOUSE

New Kid in Town

Adapted by Alice Alfonsi

Based on the series created by Marc Warren & Dennis Rinsler

Part One is based on the episode, "New Kid in Town," Written by Marc Warren & Dennis Rinsler

Part Two is based on the episode, "Ain't Miss Bahavian," Written by Marc Warren

DISNEP
PRESS

New York

First Edition
1 3 5 7 9 10 8 6 4 2

Library of Congress Catalog Card Number: 2007924557

ISBN-13: 978 1-4231-1073-6
ISBN-10: 1-4231-1073-0
For more Disney Press fun, visit www.disneybooks.com
Visit DisneyChannel.com

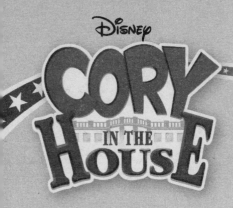

Part One

Chapter One

★★★★★★★★★★

Dang, thought Cory Baxter, as he looked out the car window. I can *not* believe I'm here!

Five days earlier, Cory and his dad, Victor, had left their San Francisco home and begun to drive across the United States. Today, they'd finally reached their destination: Washington, DC.

During his presidential campaign, Richard Martinez had stopped to eat at Mr. Baxter's restaurant, the Chill Grill. He'd loved the food so much, he'd promised Mr. Baxter a job if he won the election. Martinez had been true to his word. After he was elected, he'd asked Mr. Baxter to be the presidential chef.

Victor Baxter had decided the opportunity was too good to pass up. So now he and Cory were moving into a new house: the White House.

As Mr. Baxter stopped the car at the White House guard booth, Cory realized what a big deal it really was. He and his dad were going to be living in the same place as the commander in chief!

"Cory Baxter, reporting for duty!" he cried, as he saluted the marine sergeant on duty.

"And his dad, Victor," Mr. Baxter quickly added. He pointed to the photo on his ID card. "That's me. I'm the new White House chef. You see, President Martinez came to my restaurant and he loved my gumbo—"

"My dad uses *real* crab legs!" Cory interrupted.

"Yeah, I do," Mr. Baxter confirmed. He

paused, then switched gears. "Anyway, the president promised me that if he got elected, he would—"

Cory tapped his dad's shoulder. "Dad, the gate's open," he whispered, as he looked at the unsmiling guard. "Step on it before the man changes his mind."

"Right," Mr. Baxter agreed, hitting the gas.

A few minutes later, Mr. Baxter and Cory were carrying moving boxes into the White House.

"Man, the president hooked us up!" Cory cried, checking out their plush suite. "This place is *tight*."

Cory and his dad looked around the elegantly furnished living room. An expensive-looking rug covered a portion of the hardwood floor, a crystal chandelier hung from the ceiling, and vases of flowers rested on antique end tables. Cory paused in front of a marble fireplace.

"It's our new home, son," Mr. Baxter said, as though he still couldn't believe it. "We're living in the White House!"

Brrrriinnng!

Still holding moving boxes, Mr. Baxter and Cory looked around the luxurious room for a telephone.

"That's the hotline," Mr. Baxter realized as he spotted a red phone. "It's the president!"

Brrrriinnng!

As Mr. Baxter started toward the phone, Cory blocked his path. He had an idea. "Dad, Dad, Dad," he said calmly. "Let it ring. You don't want to seem too anxious."

Mr. Baxter hesitated, which was all Cory needed. He tossed his moving box at his father and scrambled toward the phone.

"I'll get it, Dad! Don't worry!"

"*You'll* get it?" Mr. Baxter said with surprise. He dropped both boxes and lunged after his son. They wrestled for control of the hotline, but Cory picked up the phone first.

"Don't be a wise guy!" Mr. Baxter scolded. He glared at Cory and pulled the phone out of his son's hands. Then he froze in horror. The receiver was off the hook! He hoped the president hadn't heard him.

Hesitantly, Mr. Baxter put the phone to his ear. "Uh, no, not you, Mr. President. . . . Uh, yes, Mr. President. . . . Uh-huh, of course, Mr. President. . . . Yes, I'll get right on that, Mr. President." Mr. Baxter hung up. "That was the president," he said matter-of-factly.

Cory rolled his eyes. "I got *that* part, Dad. What did he want?"

"It's my first official assignment," Mr. Baxter said proudly. "His daughter wants a hot fudge sundae."

Cory grinned and clapped his dad on the back. Mr. Baxter rushed toward the kitchen. It wasn't exactly a matter of national security, but it was obvious his dad was taking his new job seriously.

"Go, Dad, go!" Cory called. "I believe in you!"

As soon as Mr. Baxter had disappeared into the kitchen, Cory ran toward his new bedroom. He had some ideas he wanted to discuss with the president. What better time to pitch an idea than over ice cream? he thought.

Cory hurried out, the wheels of his brain already in motion.

In the kitchen, Mr. Baxter began to talk to himself. "Okay, I need ice cream, walnuts, and cherries," he said, slipping into a red chef's jacket. He scrambled around the kitchen, looking for ingredients. "Where are the cherries?" he asked, in a panic.

As Mr. Baxter frantically searched the cupboards, the president's assistant walked in. Samantha Samuels wore black-framed glasses, a blazer that looked like it had just been ironed, and a serious expression.

"Chef Victor!" she snapped.

Startled, Mr. Baxter whirled around. "What?"

Miss Samuels scanned the clipboard in her hands. "I need to know your status."

"My status?" repeated Mr. Baxter, confused. "Well, I have a lovely wife who's studying law in

England, and my daughter Raven is going to college—"

"Not your *personal* status!" Miss Samuels shouted. "The sundae, man! The sundae."

"Oh, right," said Mr. Baxter. "Momentarily. I just have to find the cherries."

As Mr. Baxter continued his search, Cory strode in carrying a briefcase. He'd changed out of his T-shirt and khakis and into his sharpest suit. "Cory Baxter, American businessman," he announced.

The president's assistant nodded crisply. "Samantha Samuels, assistant to the president."

"Put 'er there, ma'am." Cory shook Miss Samuels's hand. "You wouldn't happen to know when the president is free for a meeting?"

Miss Samuels raised an eyebrow. "With whom?"

"Cory Baxter, American businessman!" Cory replied, smoothing the lapels on his jacket. "I have some thoughts on the economy, global marketing, even a line of presidential bobble heads. . . ."

Cory snapped his briefcase open. Inside was a bobble-head doll that resembled President Martinez. Cory picked up the doll and tapped its oversize head. He nodded his own head yes along with the doll.

Miss Samuels frowned. "Let me explain to you how this works. You and your father live downstairs and take care of the kitchen. The president lives upstairs and takes care of . . . *the rest of the country.* So, as to your bobble-head agenda—" She took the doll and made it shake its head no.

Behind them, a little girl skipped toward Mr. Baxter. "Wow!" she exclaimed. "Something looks yummy!"

Cory turned and looked at her. She wore a black dress with a red ribbon around the collar, white tights, and Mary Jane shoes.

The president's assistant cleared her throat. "Chef Victor, Cory, this is Sophie, the president's daughter."

"America's angel," gushed Mr. Baxter, delighted to meet the First Daughter.

"That's what they call me," Sophie said cheerfully.

Mr. Baxter looked at the sundae. It still needed one more thing. "Now where are those cherries?" he mumbled. As he resumed his search, Sophie skipped over to Cory.

"Hey, Cory," she said. "Maybe you and I can play sometime."

Cory smiled at her. She had long, brown curls, dimples, and an adorable smile. "Look at you. You are *too* cute," Cory said. "What do you like to play?"

Sophie swished her skirt. "I like tea parties, dress up, and playing with my dollies," she replied, then looked up at Cory. "Oh, where are my manners? What do *you* like to play?"

"Well, I like video games, basketball, playing the drums—" Cory said, listing off his favorite activities.

"No," Sophie interrupted.

"No?" Cory asked, surprised.

Sophie stomped her foot. "You like tea parties, dress up, and playing with my dollies!"

Cory looked at her. Sophie was the president's daughter. I know what that means, Cory thought. What Sophie *wants*, Sophie *gets*.

"Okay," Cory said with a sigh.

Sophie waved her hand. "Don't worry, you'll catch on."

With Raven off to college and his mom in England, Cory had thought his days of being bossed around were over. Obviously, he'd thought wrong.

"Yep," Cory replied, "I'm pretty much catching on already."

Chapter Two

★★★★★★★★★★

The next morning, Cory walked through the arched doorway of his new school. Man, he thought, I'm a long way from Bayside High School—and not just in miles!

Washington Preparatory Academy was in a majestic building. The classes were small, the teachers were strict, and the students came from all over the world. The main hallway looked more like a governor's mansion than a school. Gleaming wooden staircases connected the two floors, framed portraits and stone busts decorated the walls, and muted-brown lockers were discreetly tucked away.

As students poured into the main hall, they greeted each other with hugs and stories about their summer vacations. Many wore traditional clothing from their native countries. Cory noticed that the students' clothes were even more lavish than the decor. It looked like this was where DC's rich and powerful went to school. That was okay—before long, he'd be rich and powerful, too.

"Good morning, students," a voice over the loudspeaker announced. "Welcome back to Washington Preparatory Academy—educating presidents, royalty, and future world leaders since eighteen ninety-four."

First things first, Cory told himself. Step one, find your locker.

Cory glanced at the registration card in his hand. "Eighteen," he murmured. He walked down the hall and checked the numbers on a wall of lockers. "Eighteen . . . eighteen . . ." Cory stopped. "There you are, beautiful!"

Cory opened the metal door. "Whoa," he said, surprised. "This locker comes stocked! Books, pictures, a little hand lotion. This school is swanky—yes, it is."

As Cory took out the lotion and rubbed some on his elbows, a girl approached him. "If you look in the back," she said, "I think there's some lip gloss."

"I don't really like lip gloss, you know, it makes—" Cory stopped when he saw the girl he was talking to.

"Wow," he said quietly. She was gorgeous, with thick, chestnut-colored hair, blue eyes, and a style that was totally unique. She wore dangly earrings with major-league gemstones and a pink silk dress that was wrapped around her like a sari.

"H-hi . . ." Cory's throat suddenly felt dry. "This is your locker, isn't it?" he asked.

"Yes, this is eighteen. You're in—"

"Eighteen," Cory said as he pointed to his registration card.

The girl looked at the card. With a smile, she turned it right-side up and read, "Eighty-one."

Cory felt like a total fool. "My bad," he said. "Yeah, you know, it's my first day. So—"

"But on the plus side," the girl joked, "your elbows are as soft as a baby's bottom!"

Cory laughed. Dang, he thought, she's gorgeous and funny. It's enough to make a guy forget his own name.

"I'm Meena," the girl said warmly.

"I'm . . . I'm . . ." Cory began. He suddenly realized he *had* forgotten his own name! Embarrassed, he glanced at his registration card, which he'd been nervously spinning in his hands. "I'm Y-roc."

Meena turned the card around *again*.

"I'm *Cory*," he said sheepishly.

"Well, Cory . . ." Meena paused to glance up and down the hall. "Would you mind holding this?" She held out one end of her dress.

"Not at all." Cory took hold of the material.

Meena twirled away from him, and her dress unwrapped, revealing capri jeans and a blue satin tank top. She pulled off her headband and shook out her hair. Long, brown waves tumbled down.

"My father makes me wear this stuff," she told Cory as she gathered up the pink dress. "He's the ambassador from Bahavia."

"Yeah?" said Cory. "So this little spin thing happens every day?"

"Yes." Meena stuffed her traditional Bahavian outfit into her locker and slammed the door. "And if he ever found out about this, I would be *so* grounded. Then I couldn't ride my horses."

"You have horses?" Cory asked, amazed.

Meena shrugged. "Just your basic stable."

"We have basic *cable*!" Cory said excitedly. But he could see Meena wasn't impressed. In fact, she seemed confused. "So . . . you ride horses?" Cory asked to cover his mistake.

"Oh, I just love to ride," Meena said.

"Yeah?" said Cory, waiting to hear more.

Meena nodded. "It's so much fun. The sun in my face, the wind in my hair . . ."

As she talked, Cory began to imagine riding horses with Meena.

"Cory, do you ride?" Meena asked, noticing the look on his face.

Without thinking, Cory nodded. "Uh-huh."

"What kind of horses do you have?" she asked eagerly.

"What? Uh . . ." Cory realized the conversation had taken a wrong turn, but Meena seemed so interested. He didn't want to disappoint her, so he shrugged. "The running kind. The jumping kind."

Meena clapped her hands. "You and I are going to get along great!"

Cory grinned. "I hear that!"

"Follow me," Meena said, grabbing his hand. Psyched that he already had a new friend, Cory happily followed along.

Meena led Cory down the hall, out a side door, and into a grassy courtyard. Students sat on benches and chatted as they waited for the first bell.

"This is the quad," Meena explained. "It's a nice, quiet place to study and hang out."

"Yeah," Cory replied, but he was a little confused. For a "quiet" place there was an awful lot of noise.

Wap-wap! Wap-wap! Wap-wap!

The racket was coming from above, and it was getting louder and louder. Cory looked up. A helicopter was descending on the quad.

"That helicopter's going to land right on us!" Cory cried. "Run for your lives!"

He dropped to the ground and rolled under a bench. But he seemed to be the only one who was freaked out. Everyone else just ignored the chopper.

"Cory, it's okay!" Meena yelled over the roar of the engine. "That's just my friend Newt!"

Cory peeked out from his hiding place.

"Who?" He rolled out from under the bench and stood up.

Meena pointed to a rope ladder that had been lowered from the hovering chopper. Clinging to one of the rungs was a guy with shaggy blond hair. He wore a T-shirt and blue jeans, and a guitar case was slung over his back.

"Meena!" he called, waving enthusiastically. He stepped off the ladder—and crashed to the ground.

Meena rushed over to help, but her friend had already jumped up. "That was awesome!" he said with a huge grin. Then he brushed off his T-shirt and reached out his arms. *Bam!* His book bag dropped right into them.

"Thanks, dude!" The boy waved at the chopper pilot. The ladder was pulled back up, and the helicopter flew away.

Meena gave Newt a big hug, then turned back to Cory. "This is my friend Newt Livingston."

"*Livingston?*" Cory's jaw dropped. "Like,

the Livingstons? Like, your dad's a senator and your mom's on the Supreme Court?"

"Yeah," said Newt with a shrug. "She's Chief of Justice. Or something."

"That is *cool*, man," said Cory. "Nice to meet you." He was impressed. As Cory shook Newt's hand, another boy walked up to them. He was tall and skinny, and his black hair was slicked back with gel. He wore stiff slacks, a starched dress shirt, and a narrow tie.

"Meena, how are you?" The boy took off his dark sunglasses and stared at her. "You didn't answer any of my e-mails this summer. It's almost like you were trying to *avoid* me."

"No, of course not, Jason." Meena couldn't meet his gaze. Cory guessed she wasn't telling the whole truth. "Well, maybe a little," she whispered to Cory. Then she cleared her throat and addressed Jason. "Have you met—"

"Cory Baxter," Jason interrupted as he looked Cory up and down.

Cory frowned. "How do you know my

name, bro?" he asked suspiciously.

The dude whipped out a handheld computer. "Simple face-recognition technology," he said. "It's standard issue."

"Cory, this is Jason Stickler," Meena said. "His father runs the CIA."

"Oh," Cory said, suddenly a little nervous. The Central Intelligence Agency had a lot of high-tech gadgets. They could find out anything they wanted. They probably even had his dad's secret recipe for fried chicken on file.

"So your dad's, like, the head spy?" Cory asked.

Stickler turned up the attitude. "Double-oh-*one*," he assured Cory. Then he turned toward Meena. "So, Meena, how would you like to come over tonight? I've got some satellite photos of your family vacation."

"Yeah, that's not creepy at *all* . . ." Meena whispered to Cory. "I can't," she said aloud. "The Junior Riding Club is honoring John O'Grady tonight."

"Right, right, the dinner dance at the White

House," Stickler said. He snapped his fingers. "Hey, you know what? I'll bring the photos with me."

Meena cringed. "Yikes."

"Cory, you could come too, dude," Newt said enthusiastically.

"I don't know, man," said Cory. Meena and Newt seemed nice, but Jason Stickler was a little scary. Besides, Cory had told Meena he owned horses, so he was pretty sure that an event involving horses was *not* a good idea.

"What's not to know?" Newt countered. "It's going to be a rockin' horse party!"

"Yeah?" Cory asked.

"But not a 'rocking horse' party," Newt whispered with sudden seriousness. "So *don't* bring your rocking horse." He shook his head. "I made that mistake once."

Meena spoke up. "What Newt's trying to say is you should come. You know, since you jump horses."

Cory groaned inwardly. Me and my big

mouth, he thought. I just had to say it.

"Really?" asked Stickler. He looked at Cory and narrowed his eyes suspiciously. "You're a horse jumper? Do you steeplechase?"

"Huh?" asked Cory. He had no idea what Stickler was talking about. Cory noticed the others were looking at him expectantly. "Oh, *steeplechase*. Yeah, man." He waved his hand like he was totally down with steeplechasing. After all, he didn't want to look like a fool in front of Meena. "You know, if there's a steeple around here, I'm going to be the one chasing it," Cory attempted.

Stickler elbowed Meena and smirked. Cory had obviously gotten it totally wrong. But Meena didn't seem to care what Stickler thought. "He's *joking*," she told him with annoyance. Then she turned back to Cory. "I bet you've won a lot of trophies."

"Oh, yeah," said Cory, doing his best to keep up the fake-out. "Big ol' fat ones. They even gave me a trophy for having the *most* trophies."

"Sweet!" said Newt. "So, come on. Are you going to roll with us or not?"

Cory hesitated. He didn't know the first thing about horses. Keeping up the charade for an entire evening would be a lot of work.

Then Meena put her hand on his arm. "Come on. I *promise* we'll have fun."

Suddenly Cory couldn't think of a single reason not to go to the party. "Okay," he heard himself say.

Brrrriiiiiiing!

As the school bell rang, the kids in the quad headed inside. Newt and Meena gathered their things.

"See you there!" Newt told Cory.

"Can't wait!" Meena added.

"Okay," Cory replied. He was about to go find his first class when Stickler blocked his path.

"A little word of advice," Stickler said. "Meena hates phonies."

Cory folded his arms. "What are you telling

me for?" He wasn't about to back down from anyone on his first day.

"Well, if you're *really* a horse person, then we'll find out tonight." Stickler polished his dark sunglasses. "Should be a fun evening, *champ*," he added menacingly.

Cory felt some of his confidence disappear, but he played it cool. "Yeah, *fun*," Cory said, and pretended to laugh. Stickler walked away, and Cory's laugh turned into a groan. "I'm going *down*."

Chapter Three

★★★★★★★★★

That afternoon, Cory stopped by the White House kitchen to check in with his dad. He'd planned to grab a snack, but at the moment, Cory was not feeling very hungry.

"You told them that you were a steeplechase champion?" cried Mr. Baxter. He looked horrified. "Cory, you're *afraid* of horses. You threw up on the merry-go-round!"

"Dad, that's not fair," Cory protested. "'Cause that thing was going fast, *and* up and down!"

Cory flashed back to that horrifying day out-side the supermarket. "Why'd you have to put *two* quarters in, Daddy?" he whimpered.

Mr. Baxter shook his head. Around him, the kitchen staff was busy preparing appetizers. Tonight was his first White House dinner.

Mr. Baxter folded his arms across his chef's jacket. Puzzled, he stared at his son. Cory had never liked horses. So Mr. Baxter wondered why his son had told his new classmates that he did.

"Why would you—" Mr. Baxter began, then his eyes widened with a realization. "It's about a girl, isn't it?"

"I don't know. Maybe . . . maybe . . ." Cory tried to play his dad, but the look on the man's face totally broke him. "*Yes!*" he cried. "Look, Dad, I've just got to get through tonight. I've got a couple of hours to hit the computer and learn everything I can about horses."

Cory began to walk away.

"Whoa, dude," Mr. Baxter said. "You're out of

luck. We're not getting the Internet hooked up until next week."

"Are you *serious*?" Cory asked, panicking.

With an apologetic shrug, Mr. Baxter went back to work on his appetizers.

"Man," Cory moaned, "now what am I supposed to do?"

Just then, the president's daughter skipped into the kitchen. "Hey, Cory," Sophie said. "Ready to play now?"

"I can't now, Sophie," Cory snapped. "I'm busy—" Suddenly he stopped as an idea took hold in his desperate mind.

"Sophie," Cory cooed. "America's *angel*, you wouldn't happen to have a computer upstairs, would you?"

Sophie grinned in delight. "I do. We can play computer games. I have Digital Doll Party!"

"Yo, she's got Digital Doll Party! Yo!" Cory pretended to be excited. "But you know what would be so much *more* fun than Digital Doll Party?"

"What?" Sophie asked.

"Looking up stuff about *horsies*," Cory replied.

"Horsies? Okay!" Sophie exclaimed. "I'll show you the secret passageway. C'mon!"

"Let's go!" Cory said with false enthusiasm. "Yay!" He clapped his hands. "Yay, yay, yay!"

Sophie darted out the kitchen door.

As Cory slowly followed, he shook his head. "Little kids are so easy," he mumbled. Then he laughed to himself and headed out the door.

Sophie led Cory up one set of stairs and down another, through a hallway, and into a small room that clearly wasn't hers.

Where is this girl taking me? Cory wondered.

Then, Sophie pushed open a hidden panel. She stepped through, and Cory followed. "Whoa," he whispered in awe as he looked around. "This is the Oval Office, where the president works!" He smiled.

It was just like he'd seen in photos and

books. A large, wooden desk stood in front of a tall window. There was a thick, blue carpet decorated with an American eagle. Priceless oil paintings lined the curved walls. An American flag stood in the corner, and the presidential seal was on everything.

"Are you sure we're *allowed* in here?" Cory asked.

"Well, *I* am," said Sophie.

Cory tensed. "Oh?"

"So as long as you're with *me*, you are, too," Sophie assured him.

Cory nodded with relief. "Cool."

"There's the computer." Sophie pointed toward the president's desk.

Cory sat down in the big leather chair. He stared at the presidential seal on the desk blotter. He suddenly thought about all the famous men who'd occupied this office.

"I feel the power!" he cried.

Then Cory heard footsteps approaching the office, and voices just outside the door.

"President Martinez," Miss Samuels said, "we need to talk."

"Step into my office," replied a deep voice.

"Whoa, that's your dad," Cory said, as he turned around to look at Sophie. "It's a good thing I'm with *you*." But the president's daughter was on her way out of the room.

"Have fun," Sophie called, dashing back through the secret panel.

Cory sprang from the president's chair and raced after Sophie. It was too late. The panel was closed. There was no handle on Cory's side of the wall, and he had no idea how to open the secret passage.

"Come on now," he called to Sophie as he banged on the wall. "Don't do it. Come on . . ."

Alone in the Oval Office, Cory tried not to panic. Across the room, the doorknob began to turn. He had two choices: explain or hide.

Oh, *snap!* Cory thought, I'm going with *hide*. He dove under the desk.

A moment later, President Martinez walked

into the room. "So, what's on my agenda?" he asked his assistant.

"Well, Mr. President—" Miss Samuels began.

"Ah, I love the sound of that!" the president interrupted.

"I know you do, sir." Miss Samuels sounded as if she'd heard this before.

"Well, we worked hard to get here," the president said. "We should take a moment to enjoy it." He sat in the leather chair behind his desk.

"Shall I order a balloon drop, sir?" Miss Samuels asked.

Cory began to suspect this back-and-forth was routine.

"No, no, no," said President Martinez. "That wouldn't be dignified. A simple chair spin should suffice."

The president pulled his knees up to his chin. Miss Samuels spun the chair so it twirled around like a carnival ride.

"*Woo-hoo!* We won!" the president shouted gleefully as he turned around and around.

Under the desk, Cory curled up tightly so the president's feet wouldn't hit him.

"Back to business," President Martinez said as his chair came to a stop.

"Mr. President," Miss Samuels said. "I need to speak with you about Chef Victor's son."

"What's the problem?"

"Well, sir," she said, "he has this bobble head—"

The president cut her off. "Sam, this administration will not judge people by the shape of their heads!"

Just then, the president's hound dog trotted into the room. "Hey, Humphrey," the president called. "How you doin', boy?"

Humphrey barked, then trotted under the desk. President Martinez smiled with delight. "There he goes. His favorite spot!"

"Listen up, dog," Cory whispered as the animal approached. "This is *my* spot! Get another one!"

But the dog didn't listen. He circled in place

and curled up next to Cory's feet.

"He is so affectionate," President Martinez remarked. "He could lick my hand all day." The president reached under the desk to pat the dog's head. He didn't know it was actually Cory's head!

Cory gritted his teeth. Man, he thought, this is ridiculous!

After a few minutes, the president stopped. Finally! thought Cory. But the worst was yet to come. The president held out his hand for Humphrey to lick.

Cory poked the dog. "C'mon, you do it," he whispered. But Humphrey just stared at the president's hand.

Cory rolled his eyes in frustration. Cory had no choice. If he didn't do anything, the president might look under the desk and see him there. So Cory closed his eyes in disgust, and licked the president's hand.

"Good dog!" said President Martinez. He patted Cory's head.

Meanwhile, the president's assistant stood by his desk, listening to her earpiece. "Right, got it," she said into a receiver that was pinned to her jacket lapel. Then she turned to the president. "Sir, they're waiting for you. We have that ribbon-cutting ceremony at the new bridge."

"Oh, good!" President Martinez grinned like a little boy. "I get to use the *big* scissors!"

When Cory heard the door shut, he climbed out from under the desk. Shuddering, he grabbed some tissues. As he wiped his tongue, the wall panel slid open. Sophie stepped out, laughing like crazy. She had run outside and watched everything from the window.

"Hey, Cory! How'd you like your 'hand' sandwich?" she teased.

"That was just evil," Cory told her.

"It made *me* laugh," Sophie said.

"You know what? It doesn't even matter." Cory collapsed onto a couch and shook his head in defeat. "I still don't know anything about horses, and Meena's going to know I'm a phony.

She's probably never going to talk to me again."

Sophie rolled her eyes. "Being a little dramatic, aren't we?"

"Excuse me," Cory replied, indignant. "I had to lick your dad's hand!"

"I know." Sophie looked remorseful for a moment, then she smiled. "I feel bad about that, so I got you this." She handed him a book.

Cory read the title. "*Horses for Dimwits*? This is perfect for me," he said, suddenly hopeful.

Sophie shrugged. "*I* thought so."

Chapter
Four

★★★★★★★★★

After reading *Horses for Dimwits* cover to cover, Cory felt ready to kick it with Meena and her riding friends. As the sun sank below the treetops, he put on a new blue suit and went to join the crowd at the Junior Riding Club's dinner dance.

Dozens of banquet tables were set up inside a large party tent on the White House lawn. A band played in the background. Cory noticed a banner near the front of the tent that welcomed someone named John O'Grady.

Cory joined Newt and Meena at a table. Soon, the dinner service began. Cory knew that his dad had overseen all the food preparation that night.

After the delicious dinner, kids crowded the dance floor. Cory talked horses with everyone—even Jason Stickler. Stickler gave Cory plenty of attitude and tried to trip him up again with a question about steeplechasing. This time, Cory was ready. He launched into a descriptive answer and watched Stickler become more and more annoyed.

". . . Yeah, there's something about a good ol' fashioned steeplechase," Cory continued, "which, as we *all* know, is a horse race across open country or over an obstacle course."

Meena nodded happily, and Stickler rolled his eyes.

Just then, the band began to play "Hail to the Chief."

Meena's eyes widened. "It's the president! Cory, come on!" She took Cory's hand and pulled him back to their table.

Stickler stared after them jealously. He turned toward Newt. "You realize Cory Baxter is a total phony."

Newt blinked, surprised. "I do?"

"You *will*," Stickler promised.

By now, everyone in the tent was standing and applauding President Martinez. He stepped up to the podium, and everyone sat down.

"Thank you, thank you, my fellow horse lovers," President Martinez began. "And now, it's time to welcome our guest of honor, a great champion." The president gestured to a curtain behind him. "Ladies and gentlemen, John O'Grady!" he announced.

Still in her seat, Meena leaned closer to Cory. "I can't wait to see John O'Grady in person!"

"Yeah, neither can I," Cory replied with enthusiasm. "I might even get his autograph!"

Meena looked confused. Cory wondered

why—until the curtain opened. A beautiful show horse stood tied to a post.

Oh, *snap*, Cory thought, John O'Grady isn't a man—he's a *horse*! And I just told Meena I wanted his autograph.

"You know," Cory quickly added, "if horses could write."

At the front of the tent, President Martinez waved the crowd forward. "Ladies, gentlemen, let's get a closer look."

A rider in a red jacket and black boots stepped forward and took the horse's reins. Before the man could climb into the saddle, Stickler rushed up to the microphone.

"Mr. President, ladies and gentlemen," Stickler began, "I have a surprise announcement for you all. We have a *real* steeplechase champion with us tonight!"

"Uh-oh," Mr. Baxter said under his breath. He was watching from the side of the tent.

Cory was beginning to get a bad feeling about this. "Uh-oh," he said.

"So let's bring him on up here," Stickler continued. "Cory Baxter!"

Cory frantically shook his head *no*. His new friends seemed to think he was just being shy.

"Go ahead, dude," Newt encouraged. "Chase that steeple!"

"Cory, *please*," said Meena. "If you don't, I'll be *so* disappointed."

That did it. Cory looked into Meena's big, blue eyes and knew he couldn't disappoint her. "Okay," he said. The crowd applauded as Cory walked toward the front of the tent.

On the side, President Martinez turned toward his assistant. "Is that the bobble-head boy?" he asked, pointing at Cory.

Miss Samuels nodded. "That's him, sir."

Cory took the microphone from Stickler and looked at the crowd. He racked his brain for a way out of his situation. "Ladies and gentlemen, Mr. President," Cory began, "this is quite an honor, but unfortunately I'm not exactly dressed for the occasion—"

Stickler grabbed the microphone. "Not a problem," he said with an evil grin.

A short time later, Cory found himself dressed in riding breeches, a red jacket, black boots, and a helmet that fastened with a chin strap.

Stickler had obviously planned ahead. He had made sure there was an extra riding outfit on hand. Cory had realized he couldn't back down without admitting that Stickler had found him out.

Back in the tent, Stickler pointed to the horse. "Hop on, champ," he told Cory.

The horse snorted and rolled his eyes. Cory flashed back to that day on the merry-go-round. Yo, he thought, I can *not* do this. I'm going to fall off and embarrass myself in front of all these people. If I can even figure out how to get in the saddle, Cory realized.

Then Cory saw Meena smiling at him, and he knew he had to try. Now or never, he thought, and stepped toward John O'Grady.

"Look at you," he said to the horse. "You are *much* bigger than the one at the market, aren't you? Yes, you are." He glanced at Stickler. "Got a quarter?" Cory joked nervously.

Stickler pointed to the horse. Cory wasn't exactly sure how to get on, so he tried to stall some more. "Okay, boy. All right . . . it's cool, all right?" He glanced around. "Anybody got a stepladder?"

Stickler gritted his teeth. "Get on the horse."

Cory knew this was it—the moment of truth. "It's okay, boy . . ." he said to John O'Grady. Cory put his foot into a stirrup, and heaved himself onto the horse.

Cory landed on his stomach across the saddle. He squirmed around, then managed to pull himself up into a sitting position. "All right, all right! I'm up!" he cried. He raised his arms into the air triumphantly.

Then Cory realized something wasn't quite right. "Wait . . . wait, where'd his head go?"

Oh, no, Cory realized as he noticed the

horse's tail. I'm on the horse *backward*!

Suddenly, the horse began to move. Thinking fast, Cory leaned down and gripped the horse's belly with his legs. But the horse started to walk faster.

"Okay, stop!" Cory cried, beginning to panic. "Bad horsey!"

The horse began to trot around the room. "Oh!" Cory bounced into the air, landing stomach-first across the horse's back.

Cory tried to pull himself back up, but he lost his grip and started to slide off. He did his best to stay on the horse, but he didn't know what he was doing. Soon he was hanging from the horse's neck with his arms and legs wrapped around the horse's front shoulders.

The guests watched quietly, not sure what to make of it. Newt looked impressed. "Whoa . . ." he said.

The horse kept trotting, and Cory clung to it for dear life. "*Aggghhhh!*" he screamed. "Daddy!"

Still wearing his chef's uniform, Mr. Baxter

pushed through the crowd. "Hold on, son!" he called. He tried to catch up to John O'Grady.

Stickler walked up to Newt and Meena and smirked. They both stared at the spectacle in shock.

"Cory is the chef's son?" Meena asked.

"Yep," Stickler said smugly. "Oh, and this may be obvious, but he's no steeplechase champion."

Just then, Cory and the horse swung past.

"This is worse than the merry-go-round!" Cory cried.

As Cory struggled to right himself, Meena shared a disappointed look with Newt. Then she shook her head and began to walk away.

Cory pulled himself back into the saddle and caught a glimpse of his friend leaving. "Meena! Meena, wait!" he called.

Just then, the horse stopped. Cory sighed with relief. He was still facing the horse's rear, but at least the animal wasn't moving.

"Yes!" Cory said triumphantly. "Good horsey!"

He patted the horse's rump. Before Cory could climb down, John O'Grady raised his tail.

Cory frowned. "I hope you're not doing what I *think* you're doing," he said.

Plop!

The crowd groaned as the stench wafted toward them.

Can this get any worse? Cory wondered. "Bad horsey!" he said. John O'Grady suddenly jerked forward. Cory wasn't ready. He tried to hold on, but it was no use.

"Nooooooo . . ." Cory wailed, as he slid off the horse's rear, right into the—

Splat!

"Oohhhhhh!" The crowd groaned again.

I most definitely do *not* like horses, thought Cory.

Chapter
Five

★★★★★★★★★★

Later that night, after a long, hot shower, Cory tried to sleep. But he kept dreaming he was riding a horse backward across the White House lawn while all of his classmates laughed at him.

Since he couldn't rest, Cory went looking for a midnight snack. As he walked into the kitchen, he heard someone whistling.

"Hey, I know that tune," he murmured. "It's 'Hail to the Chief.'" Then he noticed a man in a bathrobe rummaging around in the large fridge. "Mr. President?" Cory asked.

"Oh!" President Martinez jumped and hit his head on a refrigerator shelf. *"Yow . . ."* Rubbing the bruise, the president turned toward Cory. "I was just looking for some of your dad's leftover gumbo," he said, holding up a plastic bowl. "Cory, isn't it?"

"Yes, sir," Cory replied politely.

The president closed the fridge. He grabbed a spoon, then carried the bowl to the table. "I guess you had kind of a rough time tonight, didn't you?"

"You noticed, huh?" said Cory. Talk about going down in flames, he thought. Even the *president* felt sorry for him!

"Have a seat," President Martinez said.

Cory sat down. The president looked at him with concern. "Anything I can do to help?"

Cory considered. Maybe this situation doesn't have to be a total loss, he thought. It wasn't every day that a regular kid from San

Francisco had a chance to talk to the president. Of course, most kids didn't land in a pile of manure in front of the president, either. . . .

"As a matter of fact, sir," Cory began, "there is one thing. . . . I have this bobble head, right? And you know—"

"Cory, let me tell you a little story," President Martinez interrupted. "When I was growing up, there was a young boy who was the object of scorn because of the shape of his head. They called him Pumpkin Head, Basketball Head, Melon Head—"

The president shuddered as he flashed back to his childhood. Then he cleared his throat and continued.

"Well, eventually, his body caught up with that head. Of course, then people started calling him Pumpkin *Body*, but that's another story. Anyway, the point is, he made something of that head. He filled it with knowledge and passion and ambition. Because you see, Cory, that big-headed boy grew up to be . . . the *president of the United States.*" He raised his palm for a high five. "Up top."

Cory dutifully high-fived the president. "That was very inspiring, sir. It was. But, um, what about my bobble head?" Cory asked, puzzled.

President Martinez sighed. "Have you heard *anything* I've said, son? You need to hang in there. Because as bad as it feels now, if you believe in yourself, things *will* get better."

Cory was confused, but he guessed that the president was a little *more* confused about the subject of their conversation.

"Yeah . . ." Cory agreed politely. "Yeah . . . thank you, Mr. President."

Taking his bowl of gumbo, President Martinez stood up and walked toward the door. Before he left the room, he gave Cory one more piece of advice. "Keep your head up . . . if you can."

Wow, Cory thought. Who would have guessed that the president used to have a big head?

Then Cory went back to bed and caught some sleep before school.

The next day after class, Cory finally got up the courage to talk to Meena and Newt.

"Just keep your head up," Cory reminded himself as he approached the quad. Meena and Newt were chatting near a lunch table, but stopped when they saw Cory.

"Look," Cory began, "I'm sorry I lied, okay?" Then he told the whole truth. "I'm just a regular kid from San Francisco, who doesn't have a limo . . . or a helicopter . . . or know the first thing about horses. So, there." Cory anxiously waited for their reaction.

Meena and Newt exchanged glances. After a long, silent moment, Meena finally spoke.

"Come here," she said sweetly, opening her arms for a hug.

Cory couldn't believe it. Meena wasn't angry at all. It was all going to work out. He stepped up to hug her and—*pow!* She punched him in the arm.

"*Ow!*" Cory yelled. "What was that for?"

"'Cause you're a yak butt!" she shouted.

"A yak—*what*?" Cory asked, confused. He didn't know what a yak was, but more importantly, he didn't understand why Meena was angry.

"Why did you lie to us?" Meena cried. "I mean, do you think we care about that stuff?"

"Yes. I mean, I did," Cory replied. He suddenly realized what she meant. "You *don't*?"

"We just thought you were cool," Meena said with a shrug.

Newt nodded in agreement. "Yeah, a chill dude to hang with."

Cory was stunned. He'd figured everyone at this school only hung out with other rich kids. "Thanks, guys," he said with a grin. "Look, sorry we got off to a bad start. But I guess when it comes down to it, we're all just regular kids."

"Right on," Newt agreed. He held up his fist and Cory knocked it with his own.

"Yeah, man," said Cory.

Meena patted Cory's shoulder. Then she pointed to a tall guy in a chauffeur's uniform.

"My limo's here," she said. "I've got to go!"

"See ya!" Newt called after her.

Suddenly, the wind picked up.

Wap-wap! Wap-wap! Wap-wap!

"There's that helicopter!" Cory pointed toward the sky. The chopper hovered above the quad, and the pilot lowered a rope ladder. Newt hopped onto the bottom rung.

"Later, dude!" he yelled as he rose into the air. "I've got my guitar lesson . . . with Aerosmith!"

Cory shook his head. "Just regular kids," he said, as he watched Newt climb into his helicopter and fly away. "Yeah, right!"

Part Two

Chapter One

★★★★★★★★★★

The White House Press Briefing Room was crowded with TV and newspaper reporters. They chatted amongst themselves, waiting for the president to address the nation. Cameras and microphones pointed toward a wooden podium in front of a blue curtain. Both the American flag and the Bahavian flag flanked the podium.

The voices of the press dimmed to a murmur as the president's assistant, Samantha Samuels, approached the microphone. "Ladies and Gentlemen," she announced, "the President of the United States."

President Martinez walked up to the podium, and smiled at the TV cameras. "My fellow Americans," he began, "I'm happy and proud to announce, in the spirit of cooperation, two great nations have just signed a historic treaty. . . ."

A few floors away from the president, Cory Baxter sat on his living room couch watching TV.

"Dad, can you believe it?" Cory asked. "The whole world is watching President Martinez's speech, and it's happening right upstairs in our house!"

Victor Baxter was getting ready to go to work. He turned away from the mirror where he was buttoning up his chef's jacket. "Son," he said, "even though I am the new White House chef and we live in the White House, this is not really our house."

"Well, Dad, this *is* the people's house," Cory

pointed out. "And, uh, *we* the people."

Mr. Baxter sat down on the couch next to Cory to watch the president's speech.

On TV, President Martinez gestured to a gray-haired man who was wearing a high-necked white suit and a colorful sash. "I would like to thank Ambassador Rom Paroom of Bahavia for all of his hard work on this treaty, and I would like to welcome Mrs. Paroom and their daughter, Meena, to the White House."

The TV showed Mrs. Paroom and Meena standing on the side of the room next to the ambassador. The women wore traditional Bahavian wrap dresses.

"Dad, there she is!" Cory cried. "That's my friend Meena from school." He pointed toward the screen. "Check it out. She said she was going to flash us a signal to say hi."

On TV, Ambassador Paroom stepped up to the podium. "Thank you, Mr. President," he began. "We look forward to a new era of respect and understanding between our two nations."

Cory watched Meena in the background and noticed she was chewing gum. Meena began to blow a large, pink bubble. The bubble grew bigger and bigger, and then—*pop!*

"That was it! That was the signal!" Cory laughed.

On TV, however, Meena's father wasn't laughing. He gave his daughter a dirty look. Cory didn't notice. He was too excited that Meena had sent him a signal.

"How cool was that?" Cory asked his dad. "Is she the *best*? How *cute* was that bubble?"

Mr. Baxter raised an eyebrow. "I think somebody has a crush on this Meena."

Embarrassed, Cory stopped laughing. "Who? *Her?*" he said. "She's all right." Cory tried to act disinterested and turned back toward the TV. Mr. Baxter wasn't convinced. He smiled to himself and headed toward the White House kitchen.

The next morning, the president's assistant rushed into the kitchen. "Chef Victor, we have a crisis!" Samantha Samuels announced. "The president needs your help."

Mr. Baxter thought back to the president's speech the night before. He wondered if the crisis involved the treaty with Bahavia, or if it was something even more urgent.

Mr. Baxter grabbed the nearest kitchen utensils and raised them like a soldier preparing to march into battle. "Miss Samuels, I'm ready," he told her. "Whatever it takes, I'm here for my country!"

Miss Samuels looked at the skillet and whisk in Mr. Baxter's hands. "I'll be sure to call you," she said, "if we're attacked by giant *eggs*."

Embarrassed, Mr. Baxter lowered his hands and waited for Miss Samuels to continue.

"The crisis is that the president's daughter will only eat your french fries," Miss Samuels explained.

Mr. Baxter didn't quite understand. "Well, they *are* irresistibly delicious," he admitted with pride. "But I would hardly call that a crisis."

"Oh, really." The president's assistant crossed her arms over her chest. She looked annoyed. "What would *you* call a crisis?"

Mr. Baxter hesitated, then sheepishly shrugged. "If we were attacked by giant eggs?"

Miss Samuels pushed up her black-framed glasses. "Let me explain. The president needs to concentrate on running the country, and he *cannot* do so if he is worried about Sophie's obsession with your potatoes—"

She paused and listened to the miniature receiver in her ear. A secret service agent was speaking to her through the device.

"Yes. Roger that." Miss Samuels answered through a transmitter pinned to her lapel. Then she turned toward Mr. Baxter.

"Sophie's on the way down," she said. "You *cannot* give her any fries. You hear me?" She wagged her index finger at Mr. Baxter. "No fries, man. *No fries!*"

"Relax," Mr. Baxter said calmly. "I've got this taken care of, okay? I went through the same

Part One

"Man, the president hooked us up!" Cory cried.
"This place is *tight*."

"I have some thoughts on the economy,
global marketing, even a line of presidential
bobble heads…" Cory said.

"So this little spin thing happens every day?" Cory asked.

"You didn't answer any of my e-mails this summer.
It's almost like you were trying to *avoid* me," said Stickler.

"Cory, you're *afraid* of horses. You threw up on the merry-go-round!" Mr. Baxter said.

"This is the Oval Office. . . . Are you sure we're *allowed* in here?" Cory asked.

"Yeah, there's something about a good ol' fashioned steeplechase," Cory told Stickler.

"You are *much* bigger than the one at the market, aren't you?" Cory said.

Part Two

"*Remember, no fries!*" warned Samantha.

Cory tried to think of a way to cheer up Meena.

"Oh," Sophie added. "While I'm playing with this, I'm gonna want my *french fries*."

"Welcome to *casa de Newt*," said Newt. "That's Spanish for 'house *de* Newt'."

"We're not *studying*, Ambassador P," Newt explained.
"It was just an *excuse*."

"What about if we, you know, *talked* to her dad?
Let him know that we respect his culture," Cory said.

Cory and Newt joined the line of White House waiters.

"Maybe this young man, misguided as he may be, has taught us all a lesson," said the president.

phase with my own kids. Tell the president, *problem solved.*"

Miss Samuels sighed with relief. "That's what I like to hear!" As she made a note on her clipboard, the president's daughter skipped into the room.

"Good morning, Sophie," said Miss Samuels.

"Good morning, Samantha," the little girl replied politely. Sophie tossed her long, brown curls and swished her dress. "Good morning, Chef Victor."

Over Sophie's head, Miss Samuels pointed two fingers toward her own eyes then at Mr. Baxter. "*I'm watching you!*" she silently mouthed. She walked toward the door, then turned around to give Mr. Baxter a warning look. "*Remember, no fries!*"

Mr. Baxter smiled at the First Daughter, convinced that Miss Samuels was making a mountain out of a molehill.

"Good morning, Sophie," he said cheerfully. "Hey, for breakfast this morning, how about something healthy and delicious?"

"How 'bout something greasy and salty?" Sophie countered, just as cheerfully.

"How 'bout something green and leafy?" Mr. Baxter suggested a little more forcefully.

"How 'bout something brown and crispy?" Sophie countered a *lot* more forcefully.

"How 'bout something—"

"Chef Victor!" Sophie put her hands on her hips. "We can go back and forth all day, but we *both* know how this is going to end."

Mr. Baxter's face fell. "With french fries?"

Sophie grinned. "Thanks," she said sweetly. "I would love some!"

Chapter Two

★★★★★★★★★

Later that morning, Cory was hanging at his school locker with his new friend Newt Livingston. Meena rushed up to them.

"Guys, did you see me last night?" she asked.

Cory nodded. "You were *beautiful*," he said with a dreamy grin. Then he saw Meena give him a strange look and tried to cover. The last thing Cory wanted was to embarrass himself in front of Meena.

"I mean, you know," Cory corrected himself, "that *bubble* was beautiful."

Meena turned toward Newt expectantly. He looked puzzled. "Wait . . . did you see *me*?" Newt asked.

Meena rolled her eyes. "Uh, Newt, TV doesn't work that way."

"Oh, good," Newt said with relief. "'Cause I was in the bathtub."

Cory decided it was time to move the conversation along. "Anyway . . ." he said, "I got you a CD." He handed Meena a plastic jewel case.

Meena read the handwritten title on the CD. "*Cory's Hot Jamz*?"

Cory was expecting Meena to be excited. He was surprised that she actually looked sort of bummed. "Oh, well," he said, disappointed. "If you don't like it, I'll take it back—"

Cory reached for the CD, but Meena pulled it away. "No," she said firmly. "This is so sweet."

Seeing Cory's confused expression, Meena

tried to explain. "It's my father. He's been on my case lately." She sighed, obviously upset. "He gave me this whole lecture about how good Bahavians do not chew gum in public, and how I'm losing my culture. How can he say that?" she cried. Meena paused to untuck the end of her dress and hand it to Cory. "Help me unwrap."

Cory dutifully took hold of the silk. Meena spun into the center of the hallway. Her traditional Bahavian dress unwrapped, revealing a blue T-shirt, white jeans, and a rhinestone-studded belt.

"Hey," said Newt, pointing down the hall. "Isn't that your dad?"

They all turned to look.

Ambassador Paroom was walking through a crowd of students. He wore a Bahavian tunic and a pinched expression. He was obviously looking for Meena.

Meena looked panicked. "Rewrap! Rewrap!" she cried frantically.

Meena spun in reverse and covered up her trendy clothing with her Bahavian wrap. A moment later, Ambassador Paroom walked up to them.

Cory could see that Meena's father did not look happy.

Newt noticed, too, and tried to lighten the mood. "What's crackin', Ambassador P?" he asked, grinning broadly.

The ambassador frowned at Newt. "Hello, Newton," he replied.

"Father, is there a problem?" Meena asked worriedly.

"Meena, you left your yak backpack in the limousine." The ambassador held up a pack made of white shaggy fur, bells, and horns. "You're not ashamed of this, are you?" he asked sharply.

Ambassador Paroom shook the pack, its bells jingling loudly like a sleigh coming down the hall. He handed the pack to Meena, and she cringed with embarrassment.

"No, Father. Of course I'm not ashamed," Meena said. "It is the nicest gift that Grandma Paroom ever skinned for me." She smiled weakly.

The ambassador looked suspicious. As he studied Meena's expression, he noticed the CD in her hand. "What is *this*?" he asked. Before Meena could stop him, her father snatched the case. The ambassador's eyes narrowed as he read the title.

"It's just some music," Meena said defensively.

"*Cory's Hot Jamz*?" Ambassador Paroom held up the CD. "Who is this *Cory*? And why are his *jamz* so hot?"

Ambassador Paroom looked upset. Cory, sure the man would chill once he heard what was on the CD, stepped forward.

"I'm Cory, sir," he began confidently. "The secret to my little mix is a little old school, a little new school, and just a sprinkle of funk. You know what I mean?"

The ambassador's expression soured. He handed the CD to Cory. "Thank you," he said, "but you can keep your *funky sprinkles*. Meena has plenty of traditional Bahavian music at home."

"But, Father," Meena pointed out, "how many times can we listen to *Ickbob: Master of the Nose Flute*?"

The ambassador clenched his fists. "He is the master for a reason!" he cried. Realizing he seemed angry, he took a deep breath and gritted his teeth. "I will talk to you at home," he warned his daughter.

"Later, Ambassador P!" Newt said.

Meena's father glared. "Newton," he mumbled, then marched away.

When the ambassador was out of earshot, Cory turned toward Meena. "Sorry about the CD," he said apologetically. "I didn't mean to get you in trouble."

"It's not your fault," said Meena. "I just wish that I didn't have to hide such a big part of my life from him. He's so old-school Bahavian."

Meena looked angry and sad at the same time. Cory tried to think of a way to cheer her up, but he couldn't. Luckily, Newt came to the rescue. "Yeah, my dad's the same way," he said. "Except he was born in Ohio, and surprisingly, he loves him some funk."

Meena smiled, then she turned toward Cory. "I want the CD," she said.

"Are you sure?" Cory asked doubtfully.

Meena nodded and took the CD from him. "It's either this or Nose Flute–apalooza." Meena made a face. "Help me unwrap!"

Once again, Cory took hold of the silk. Meena spun around and eagerly shed her traditional Bahavian outfit.

Later that day, Miss Samuels marched into the White House kitchen. "Chef Victor, I need to know where we stand," she demanded.

"Well," said Mr. Baxter. He wiped his hands

on a tea towel, stalling for time to think of the right answer. "I thought we were getting along, but sometimes I feel a little tension between us—"

"Not our relationship!" the president's assistant cried. "Sophie. French fries. Crisis? Any of this ring a bell?"

"Uh, yeah," said Mr. Baxter uncomfortably. He considered explaining that he had tried to feed Sophie a healthy breakfast, but she'd refused to eat anything but french fries. "We sort of hit a little bump in the road."

"What?" screeched Miss Samuels. "The president will be very disappointed. I told him problem solved!"

Mr. Baxter frowned. "Why did you tell him that?"

"Because you said, and I have the quote right here . . ." She flipped to a page on her clipboard and read: "Tell the president 'problem solved.'"

"And it will be," Mr. Baxter quickly assured her. He was stunned—she had written down their conversation? "I still have a few tricks up my sleeve and—"

Miss Samuels picked up her pen and started taking notes.

"Stop writing that down!" Mr. Baxter cried.

She put down her pen reluctantly. "Well, your tricks better work," she warned. "Sophie's joining the president at the ambassador's dinner tonight, and he will not want to see her eating french fries." Miss Samuels paused and listened to her earpiece. "Yes, roger that," she replied, then looked at Mr. Baxter. "She will be here in three, two, one . . ."

The president's daughter skipped into the kitchen.

"Hi, Sophie!" Miss Samuels said cheerfully.

"Hello. What's for lunch?" Sophie asked sweetly. Her bright eyes darkened. "I hope it rhymes with *mench mies*."

"Uh, Sophie, I have a big surprise for you," Mr. Baxter said as he pointed toward the kitchen table. A red tablecloth covered something wide and lumpy. Mr. Baxter pulled off the cloth with a flourish.

Sophie rushed over to see her surprise. A large silver tray held a miniature farm made out of healthy foods. Mr. Baxter had made a pretzel-stick windmill, a cheese tractor, and farm animals from fruits and vegetables.

"Wow, it's a farm made out of delicious-looking vegetables!" Sophie exclaimed.

Mr. Baxter nodded proudly and picked up an animal from the tray. "I'm a cauliflower *sheeeeeeep*," he said, imitating a bleating sheep.

Sophie laughed. "That's so cool!" She clapped her hands and sat down.

Mr. Baxter grinned as the First Daughter played with the vegetable farm. "Problem solved," he whispered to Miss Samuels, then snapped his fingers.

The president's assistant looked like she was *almost* convinced.

"Oh," Sophie added. "While I'm playing with

this, I'm going to want my french *fries*."

Miss Samuels glared at Mr. Baxter. Then she took the cauliflower sheep from his hand and lifted it to eye level. "This is very *baaaaaaad*."

Mr. Baxter couldn't have agreed more.

Chapter
Three

★★★★★★★★★

After school, Cory went to Newt's house to hang out. Meena had said she'd try to meet up with them later.

"Come on in," Newt said as they stepped through the back door. "Welcome to *casa de Newt*. That's Spanish for 'house . . . *de* Newt.'"

Wow, thought Cory, Newt's *casa* isn't as big as the White House—but it sure is close.

Then again, the dude's dad was a senator, and his mom was on the Supreme Court, so it made sense that their house was amazing.

Newt led the way into his music room. Cory couldn't believe his eyes. Was this guy for real? he wondered. The huge space was filled with guitars, a neon-lit jukebox, and edgy rock 'n' roll posters. There was even a raised stage.

"Your music room is tight!" Cory said with excitement. Then he noticed a set of drums. "Your kit is sweet! I had to leave mine back in San Francisco."

Cory climbed onto the stage for a closer look. He saw a set of drumsticks and picked them up.

"Go ahead," Newt offered. "Make some noise."

"Are you sure?" Cory didn't want to get Newt in trouble with *his* parents, too.

Newt waved his hand. "I had the room soundproofed so I can't hear my parents."

Cory didn't need to be asked twice. He could hold his own on the drums. He sat down at the drum set and played a slammin' beat.

"Man, the kid's still got it!" Cory cried, and finished with a cymbal crash. "You know what I'm saying?"

"Hey, guys!" Meena said as she walked through the back door.

"Cool!" Cory exclaimed. "You made it."

Meena threw her Bahavian wrap over a chair. "Yes, but my father thinks I'm here to study." She made a face, wrinkling up her nose.

"Oh, man," Newt complained. "Now we've got to *study*?" He'd been planning to just hang out.

"That's just an *excuse*," Meena explained, rolling her eyes. Then she turned toward Cory. "I listened to the CD you made. I loved that third cut, 'I Want to Be More Than Friends.'"

"Yeah," Cory replied with a shy smile. He'd picked that one out especially for her. "I was hoping you'd feel that one."

"I love that song," Newt chimed in. "The guitar on that is epic. Check this out."

Newt strapped on one of his many electric

guitars and flipped on the giant amps. He wailed on the guitar strings.

Newt is pretty good, thought Cory.

Cory followed the beat and put the drumsticks in motion. He looked over at Meena. She listened for a few bars, then started swaying to the music.

"Nice," said Newt. "Let's kick it up a notch!"

Cory nodded. "Let's do it, man!"

Newt flipped a few switches. Colorful strobe lights began to flash around them. A microphone rose up from the stage floor.

Cory grinned. That was pretty cool, he thought.

Meena danced over to the mike, and began to sing. Then she jumped and tossed her long hair around. She was really rockin' out!

Cory was surprised. She seemed totally different than "school Meena."

Meena sang the lead, and Cory and Newt backed her up on the drums and guitar.

The three friends played hard, really jamming

to the music. Then, right in the middle of the song—

"*Meena!*"

Ambassador Paroom's voice boomed over the music. Newt, Cory, and Meena froze.

Oh, no, Cory thought. This can't be good.

Ambassador Paroom had been spying on Meena through the window. When he'd seen her singing, he had charged through the door. Now he began to scold his daughter.

"Why are you dressed like that?" he demanded angrily. "Dancing to that wild music? Is this how you study?" Sheepishly, Meena stepped down from the stage. Her father glared at her.

Newt hopped down, still holding his guitar. He shook his head. "We're not *studying*, Ambassador P," he said, trying to clear things up. "It was just an *excuse*."

Meena waved her hands for Newt to be quiet. But it was too late. The ambassador's face got redder than Newt's neon lights.

"I knew something was wrong when I found that *Hot Jamz* CD in the Ickbob case!" Meena's father cried.

Cory thought things were getting out of hand. A little Baxter charm should smooth this right out, he thought. He stepped forward. "Sir, if I may—"

"You may not!" shouted the ambassador.

"Okay," said Cory, stepping back.

"*You* are the reason my daughter is not behaving like a Bahavian," the ambassador said to Cory.

"*Me?*" Cory said with surprise. "What did I do? I didn't—"

"Silence!" Meena's father shouted. Startled, everyone jumped as the word echoed through the room. "*Silence . . . silence . . . silence . . .*"

"Whoa, my bad," said Newt. "I accidentally hit the reverb button." He flipped a switch on the amp and calmly turned back to Meena's father. "Continue with your tirade."

"My 'tirade' is over," the ambassador replied

stiffly. "And *you*, Newton. All these years I thought you were merely a harmless distraction!" He shook his head with disappointment.

"Wait," said Newt, confused. "I thought your tirade was over."

"Enough!" The ambassador turned toward his daughter. "Meena, these boys have no respect for our culture. You are *forbidden* to talk to them *ever* again."

Meena was devastated. "Father, *please* . . ." she begged. Her eyes filled with tears, but Ambassador Paroom wasn't moved.

"Meena, we are going home—*now!*" he cried. "*Now . . . now . . . now . . .*" his voice echoed.

Cory turned to Newt. "Man, will you please stop hitting that stupid reverb button!"

"That's not me. He's just that mad!" cried Newt. "*Mad . . . mad . . . mad . . .*" Newt's voice echoed.

Cory glared.

"Oh," Newt said sheepishly. "Maybe it *was* me."

Meena gathered up her things. She looked sadly at Cory and Newt, then followed her father out the door.

Cory felt awful—he hadn't meant to get Meena in trouble. *Man, her dad is strict!* he thought. He paced back and forth. "Is Meena's dad *serious*? Like, she can never speak to us again?"

"Dude, what part of 'forbidden' don't you understand?" Newt replied. "'Cause for me, it's the *idden*."

Cory stopped pacing, and stared at Newt. "Man, how does your brain *work*?" he asked. Then he realized he didn't really want to know.

"Listen, just *focus*, okay?" Cory continued. "What about if we, you know, *talked* to her dad? Let him know that we respect his culture."

Newt nodded enthusiastically. "Yeah! That's perfect!"

"Yeah," Cory agreed. Then he frowned. "I just wish we *knew* something about his culture. That way we could respect it."

Newt grinned and jerked his thumb toward his chest. "Dude, I've been to Bahavia with Meena. Our families went there together on vacation."

"That's perfect, man!" Cory clapped his hands. "So you can fill me in." He looked at Newt expectantly.

"Totally," said Newt. Then he looked puzzled. "But we still have to get to Ambassador P."

Cory thought about it for a minute, then snapped his fingers. "He's coming over for dinner at the White House tonight, man."

"Perfect. Yeah!" Newt gave Cory a high five. Then his face fell. "But we're not invited."

Cory grinned and put an arm around Newt's shoulders. He wasn't about to let a little thing like an invitation get in his way. Watch the master and learn, he thought.

"Let me explain to you how I do . . ." said Cory.

Oh, yeah, Cory thought. Operation Crash White House Dinner is going to be a snap.

Chapter Four

★ ★ ★ ★ ★ ★ ★ ★ ★

That night, the White House kitchen was buzzing as Mr. Baxter and his staff prepared for the ambassador's dinner. It was nearly time for the meal to begin, and Mr. Baxter was nervous. He wanted everything to be perfect. Mr. Baxter began to inspect the appetizers that were lined up on the counter.

"Perfect!" he declared and passed the first plate to a waiter, who carried it out to the dining room.

"Next!" Mr. Baxter yelled.

Another waiter stepped forward. Mr. Baxter inspected an appetizer plate. "Perfect!" he said. "Next!"

Mr. Baxter inspected a third, a fourth, and a fifth plate, and handed each one to the next waiter in line. "Perfect! Next! . . . Perfect! Next! . . . Perfect! Next!"

While the inspection process continued, Cory and Newt joined the line of White House waiters. Nobody noticed because they were dressed in black pants, starched white shirts, bright blue jackets, and bow ties—just like the real waiters.

"Perfect! Next! . . . Perfect! Next!" Mr. Baxter continued to shout.

Then it was Newt's turn. As he stepped forward, Newt held a silver serving tray in front of his face.

Cory was right behind his friend. Don't look up, don't look up, Cory thought. Mr. Baxter was so focused on the food, he didn't even notice when he handed his own son a plate. Phew! Cory thought. Okay, let's find the exit!

Cory rushed toward the kitchen door, but Newt stopped right in front of him.

Dude, what are you doing? Cory wondered. Let's go, let's go! He was sure that any minute his dad would bust them.

Then Newt picked up an appetizer from his tray and took a bite. Cory panicked. He slapped Newt's white-gloved hand and pushed him through the double doors.

When Cory saw the White House dining room, he hesitated. I'm glad I'm in a waiter's tux, he thought, or I'd be seriously under-dressed! A long table was covered with a white linen cloth, and set with china plates and crystal glasses. The room was lit by an antique chandelier and decorated with fresh flowers.

Cory saw Meena standing near her mother and father. The Parooms were mingling with the other guests and wore traditional Bahavian outfits.

Just then, the band began to play "Hail to the Chief." Two secret service agents in dark suits walked into the room and held the doors ajar. A moment later, the president entered, accompanied by his daughter, Sophie. Close behind was the president's assistant, Miss Samuels.

As everyone applauded, Cory pulled Newt to the back of the room. They needed to review their game plan.

"Okay, now look," Cory whispered. "Once everyone sits down to eat, I'm going to head over to the ambassador and work my magic."

"Cool," said Newt. "Now remember, in Bahavia a traditional greeting is a hug and a kiss on both cheeks."

No problem, thought Cory. I've got this.

Across the room, Miss Samuels pulled President Martinez aside and gave him some last-minute instructions.

"Now remember, Mr. President," she said, "Bahavians frown upon any physical contact in public. It's considered very disrespectful."

The president nodded. "Got it. No physical contact."

"And remember," Samantha added seriously, "making eye contact with another man's wife is considered very rude."

In the opposite corner of the room, Newt gave Cory advice on the proper way to greet Mrs. Paroom. "You've just got to look her in the eye," Newt said. "Okay?"

Cory nodded. Just wait till Newt saw him in action.

"Oh," Newt added, "and give her a little tickle under the chin."

Meanwhile, Miss Samuels was just finishing up. ". . . Because their prisons are filled with chin ticklers."

"Who would even think of doing something like that?" President Martinez wondered aloud.

Over in the corner, Cory practiced his chin-tickling technique on Newt.

Newt nodded in approval. "Exactly. Just like

that." He grinned. "I think you're ready."

"I think so," Cory agreed. He watched the president cross the room to greet the ambassador and his family. After a moment, the president turned toward the rest of his guests.

"Ladies and gentlemen," President Martinez announced, "Ambassador Paroom and I are delighted you could join us tonight to celebrate our treaty and to enjoy a great meal prepared by our new White House chef, Victor Baxter."

Cory's dad walked into the room and waved to the guests. Everyone applauded. Cory felt a burst of pride and began to wave to his dad. Then Cory remembered that he wasn't supposed to be there, and ducked down out of sight.

After his moment in the spotlight, Mr. Baxter started to walk back to the kitchen. Then he saw Sophie wave. Already seated at the table, she beckoned him over.

"Chef Victor," Sophie said, pointing to her plate of vegetables. "I don't see my french fries."

"Sophie, I am putting my foot down," Mr. Baxter said firmly. "I'm an adult, and you are a child, and I say, *no more french fries*."

"Okay," Sophie said innocently. She crossed her arms. "I'm telling my daddy that you *yelled* at me."

Mr. Baxter panicked. "No, no, no, no!" he begged as the president's daughter pretended to cry.

"*Waaaaah!*"

Mr. Baxter was desperate. He picked up a napkin and folded it into a shape. Then he made it hop in the air. "Sophie, look at the bunny. Look at the bunny. Come on!"

A napkin bunny? Sophie thought. Puh-lease. "French fries! *Waaaaah!*" she wailed.

"Okay, *fine*," Mr. Baxter snapped, losing patience. "I'll heat up the grease."

Instantly, Sophie stopped crying. "Thank you," she said sweetly.

Mr. Baxter sighed in defeat and trudged back into the kitchen.

By that time, the president had finished greeting his guests. He walked to the head of the dining table. "Now, if you'd all be seated . . ." he said.

Everyone took their seats.

"I have a little surprise," President Martinez continued. "It gives me great pleasure to welcome Bahavian superstar, Ickbob, master of the nose flute!"

Ambassador Paroom gave a little shout of delight. He applauded loudly when Ickbob appeared. When the applause died down, the musician tossed back his long, gray hair, raised a wooden flute to his nose, and began to blow.

On the other side of the table, Meena rolled her eyes. "It's bad enough I have to listen to these lame nose tunes on CD at home," she grumbled to herself. "Now I've got to listen to them *live!*"

President Martinez smiled politely while Ickbob played. Then he turned in his seat to check on his daughter. He noticed she hadn't touched her appetizer plate.

"Don't these vegetables look yummy, honey?" he whispered.

"I guess," Sophie said with a shrug, "but I told Chef Victor to make me some—"

Miss Samuels was right behind the president. "Uh, sir!" she quickly interrupted. She didn't want the president to know Sophie still wouldn't eat anything but french fries. She had already told him the problem was solved. She pretended to get a message through her earpiece. "There is a situation!" she cried.

The president frowned. "Where?"

"Uh . . ." Miss Samuels thought fast. "The *Situation* Room."

"Makes sense." President Martinez smiled at his guests as he stood up. "Be right back, everyone."

Ickbob stopped playing.

"Enjoy those nose tunes," the president said. Then he glanced at Ickbob. "Keep blowing."

Cheerful Bahavian flute music filled the room again as Miss Samuels hustled the president toward the door.

Cory decided it was time to make his move. Ambassador Paroom looked like he was in a good mood. Must be enjoying those nose tunes, Cory thought as he carried a silver tray around the dining room.

Just then, Meena looked up and noticed Cory and Newt dressed as waiters.

Meena looked around at the other guests, who were chatting amongst themselves. She rose from her chair and made her way around the table to Newt, who was serving appetizers. "What are you guys doing here?" she asked.

Newt pointed across the room. Cory was walking over to Ambassador Paroom. "Cory's going to show your dad how much we respect your culture," Newt replied.

Meena frowned. "But he doesn't know anything about my culture." She looked concerned.

"Don't worry." Newt grinned. "I briefed him."

"You *what*?" Meena turned back to look at Cory. She had to stop him.

Cory tapped Ambassador Paroom on the shoulder. Meena's father looked up from his seat. Instantly, his face went dark. Uh-oh, Cory thought, he looks mad again.

"*You!*" the ambassador said.

"Sir, I'm sorry we got off on the wrong foot," Cory quickly said, "but I'm here to let you know that I *respect* your culture, and I'm going to show it."

Cory remembered exactly what Newt had said—in Bahavia, a traditional greeting was a hug and a kiss on both cheeks. Cory pulled Meena's dad out of his seat, then hugged him tightly and kissed his cheek.

"What are you doing?" cried Ambassador Paroom. He looked horrified.

What did I do wrong? Cory wondered. Wait, of course. "Oh, I'm so sorry, sir," said Cory. "I forgot the other cheek!" He kissed Meena's father again. The ambassador stared in shock.

Across the room, Meena was just as stunned. "Why is he kissing my father?" she asked Newt.

Newt shrugged. "Because I told him that's how Bahavians say, 'What's up.'"

"*No!*" Meena said, upset. "That's how Bahavians get *locked* up!"

"What are you talking about?" asked Newt, suddenly serious. "I was there with you on vacation. You have that relaxed island lifestyle."

"Newt, we weren't in Bahavia!" Meena cried. "We were in the *Bahamas*!"

"Oh. Right," said Newt, sheepishly. Suddenly, he remembered. He nodded and smiled. "Good times."

Meena glared.

Chapter
Five

★★★★★★★★★

"This is an outrage!" Ambassador Paroom shouted.

"I am *so* sorry, sir," Cory replied. "Where are my manners? I forgot the missus."

Cory turned toward Mrs. Paroom and pulled her up from her seat. He looked her right in the eye, just as Newt had advised. Mrs. Paroom tried to avoid his gaze, but Cory didn't give up until he was able to lock eyes with her.

Meena's mother tried to pull away. "You

are looking in my eyes!" she objected.

"Yes, I'm trying to," said Cory, confused. Wasn't this part of the Bahavian custom? he wondered. "Now let me see those beautiful peepers!" He turned Mrs. Paroom by the shoulders and stared into her eyes.

Meena rushed across the room. "Cory, no!" she shouted.

Cory figured that Meena didn't understand what he was doing. Wait till she sees this! he thought. "Meena, I got this! Watch," he said. "Ready?"

Cory tickled Mrs. Paroom's chin. The other guests gasped loudly.

"My chin!" cried Mrs. Paroom. "My sacred chin!"

Cory began to get the feeling he'd done something wrong. Why was everyone so upset?

Just then, Mrs. Paroom fainted and fell forward. Her arms landed around Cory's neck.

"Hey, hold up, lady!" Cory cried. "I don't know you like that!"

Cory was afraid to drop Mrs. Paroom, so he held her up as best he could.

The ambassador was furious. "Get your hot jamz off my wife!" he shouted.

Cory let go of Meena's mother, but she didn't fall. Her bracelets had tangled together, and her arms were locked around Cory's neck. He walked backward, but Mrs. Paroom went with him.

"Cory!" Meena shouted from across the room. "Newt made a mistake. He's never been to Bahavia!"

"Yeah, it was the *Bahamas*," Newt explained. "Kinda funny, huh?"

Cory couldn't believe it. "I'm not laughing!" he replied, struggling to loosen Mrs. Paroom's arms.

"Get out!" Ambassador Paroom yelled at Cory.

"Okay, okay. I'm going," said Cory. He moved toward the door, but Mrs. Paroom followed.

"Not with my wife!" yelled Ambassador Paroom. He rushed up to Cory and tried to pry his wife's arms loose. But her bracelets were stuck.

"Cory, let go of my mother!" Meena said.

"I'm trying!" Cory replied. "Her bracelets are locked. I can't get out!"

"Enough of this!" shouted Ambassador Paroom. He stepped behind Cory and tried to unhook his wife's bracelets. Several dinner guests rose from the table to help.

Meanwhile, President Martinez was returning to the dining room. "Weird that there was no situation in the Situation Room," he told his assistant as they walked down the long hall.

"Maybe we should rename it, sir," Miss Samuels said with a nervous shrug.

"Sam, what's going on?" the president asked.

Miss Samuels hated to admit failure, but the truth was bound to come out eventually. Sophie was still eating nothing but french fries. The president had to be told.

"The truth is, sir," Miss Samuels admitted as

she opened the dining room door, "I didn't want you to see—"

"Sophie's eating her vegetables!" cried the president.

"She *is*?" Miss Samuels looked into the dining room. Sophie sat at the table. As she munched carrots and celery, she watched something across the room.

"This is an insult to my country, my culture, and my family!" shouted Ambassador Paroom.

Miss Samuels and the president turned in the opposite direction, and saw Cory and Mrs. Paroom tangled together. Ambassador Paroom looked furious.

"Now *that's* a situation," the president said to his assistant. He rushed forward to help.

At that moment, the ambassador pulled his wife's arms, and her bracelets untangled. Meena's father lost his balance and toppled to the floor.

I'm free—finally! thought Cory. Then he saw Meena's dad on the floor. Oops! he thought. That's not good.

The president rushed over and reached out a hand. "Mr. Ambassador, allow me to help you up!" He grabbed the ambassador's hand.

Miss Samuels gasped. "No physical contact!" she reminded the president.

"Right, right!" President Martinez quickly let go of the ambassador's hand, and the man fell backward onto the floor.

"*Ahhh!*"

The president leaned over. "Mr. Ambassador, I'm sure there's an explanation for this. And I promise I will launch a full investigation."

"There is nothing to investigate!" Meena's father scrambled to his feet and brushed himself off. "My wife and I were attacked by a maniac."

Cory expected the ambassador to be a little ticked off, but he looked like he was going to blow. Before Cory could think of something to say, Meena stepped forward.

"Father, he's not a maniac. He's my friend," Meena said. "Cory was just trying to reach out and show that he respects our culture."

"By mocking it?" asked the ambassador.

"Well, he may have gotten some bad advice," Meena explained. She pointed to Newt, who nodded.

"Sorry about that, Ambassador P."

"The point is, Cory had the courage to face you," said Meena, "which is something I've never been able to do."

Ambassador Paroom frowned. "Meena, what do you mean?"

"The truth is, I have been living two lives and hiding one from you," she confessed sadly. "And I don't want to do that anymore."

Meena's father sighed. "Is that what living in this country has done to you?"

President Martinez cleared his throat. "Mr. Ambassador, Mrs. Paroom, if I may . . ." Using his most presidential voice, he declared, "You have a beautiful, talented, accomplished daughter. She embodies the best of *your* culture and of *our* culture. And, well, isn't that what our treaty is all about? Maybe this young man . . ." He put his arm around Cory. ". . . misguided as he may be, has taught us all a lesson."

As the ambassador considered the president's words, Cory spoke up. "Yeah, thank you, Mr. President. You know, I'd just like to say that—"

The president tightened his grip on Cory's shoulder. *Really* tightened it.

"Mr. President," Cory said through gritted teeth, "you know, it's pretty hard to talk when I'm in *pain*."

"That's the idea, son," the president replied quietly. "Just keep smiling, and we *may* get through this."

Maintaining his grip on Cory, President Martinez quickly turned to the nose flute master. "Ickbob," he called, "take us home."

Ickbob picked up his nose flute and began to play. Everyone swayed to the Bahavian music.

Cory snuck a glance at Meena, who smiled at him around her dad's shoulder. Yes! Cory thought proudly. *I knew the Baxter charm would save the day.* He smiled, then winced as his shoulder twinged. *Man,* he thought, *the prez has got* some *grip!*

Chapter Six

★★★★★★★★★

The next morning, Cory caught up with Newt on the quad.

"Man," said Cory, checking his watch. "It's almost time for class and still no sign of Meena. You think her dad pulled her out of school?"

Newt shook his head. "That would be a serious bummer."

"I know, man," said Cory. "We *just* became friends. There's so much I wish I had the chance to say to her."

"Hi, guys!" called Meena.

The boys turned around. Meena walked across the lawn toward them. For the first time, she'd come to school dressed in her American clothes.

"Meena!" Newt cried in surprise. He quickly turned to elbow Cory. "Now's your chance, dude," he whispered.

Cory hesitated.

"Cory's got some things to say to you," Newt told Meena as she joined them.

Cory suddenly felt tongue-tied. "H-hey . . . I . . . uh-uh . . ." he stammered.

Newt nodded with a serious expression. "Wish I had said that."

Cory rolled his eyes. "Meena, why are you talking to us?" he asked. "And where's your wrap?"

"I don't have to wear it to school anymore," Meena explained. She seemed happy.

"Yeah?" Cory asked, surprised. "And that's okay with your dad?"

"Well . . ." Meena sighed. "I still have to carry my yak backpack."

"Cool," said Newt. "So everything's copacetic?"

Meena nodded, then smiled at her friends. "He wasn't very happy that I've been keeping secrets," she explained, "but thanks to you guys and the president, he's starting to see that being part of two cultures can be a good thing."

"Yeah, like Chinese food and chocolate milk!" Newt exclaimed.

Say *what*? Cory thought. In what universe do those two things go together? Right—*Newt's* universe.

"Oh, man," Newt complained, "now I'm hungry."

Meena smiled. "So you guys want to jam after school? My dad said it would be cool."

"Really?" Cory could hardly believe his ears.

"Well, he didn't actually use the word *cool*," Meena admitted. "What he said was—" She stomped her foot and shook her fist. "'*Be home by six and don't disgrace me!'"* Then she laughed. "But that's cool for him."

"Sorry, I've got to pass," Cory said, disappointed. "My dad grounded me."

"Why?" asked Meena, puzzled.

"Something about almost causing an international incident." Cory shrugged. Parents! he thought grumpily.

"I'm grounded, too," said Newt. "Something about *helping* a guy almost cause an international incident."

"Man, that's tough," said Meena, hiding a smile. "Your parents are *soooooo* strict."

"Oh, you got jokes now?" Cory teased. "I see how it's gonna be."

Brrrriiiiiinnnng!

Newt jumped. "What was that?" He looked around.

"That's the school bell," said Cory.

"Good," said Newt with relief, "so you heard it, too."

Cory shook his head with a smile. The dude

seriously needed to turn down the amps a notch or two. Cory was glad everything had worked out for Meena, but he couldn't wait till *he* wasn't grounded. He had some serious rockin' out to do with his new friends!

Meanwhile, back at the White House, Cory's dad was about to get his own surprise. Miss Samuels had come down to the White House kitchen to give Mr. Baxter an update on Sophie.

"So, Sophie ate all her vegetables last night, huh?" Mr. Baxter said with a proud grin. "I knew she couldn't resist my cooking. Mission accomplished!"

Miss Samuels leaned against the kitchen counter. "Actually, Chef Victor, it wasn't your cooking. Sophie was so distracted by the excitement, she didn't realize what she was eating."

Mr. Baxter's grin disappeared. "So what are you saying?" he asked.

"Well . . ." Samantha checked her notes. "The president wants us to continue . . . Operation

Distract Sophie So She'll Eat Something Other Than French Fries."

Mr. Baxter sighed. He definitely had a bad feeling about this.

At Miss Samuels's instruction, he prepared a healthy meal of fruits and vegetables. Then Ickbob, master of the nose flute, came back to the White House for another command performance—this time, in the kitchen.

At noon, Sophie arrived for lunch. As soon as she sat down at the table, Mr. Baxter and Miss Samuels began to dance to Ickbob's music. Then, distracted by the funny sight of the chef and the president's assistant dancing, Sophie began to eat her vegetables.

After fifteen minutes, Mr. Baxter was exhausted. He threw up his hands and leaned against the counter. Miss Samuels was tired, too. She slumped beside him.

Suddenly, Sophie wasn't distracted anymore. She looked down at her plate. "Hey!" she cried. "These aren't french fries!"

Mr. Baxter shook his head. He clapped his hands at Ickbob. Then Mr. Baxter and Miss Samuels went back to dancing—and Sophie went back to eating.

Oh, *man*, thought Mr. Baxter. I knew working in the White House kitchen would have its challenges. But I *never* thought I'd have to get down to a nose flute!

Sneak a peek at the next
Cory in the House book. . . .

Top Secret!

Adapted by Alice Alfonsi

Based on the series created by Marc Warren & Dennis Rinsler

Based on the episode, "Beat the Press," Written by Dennis Rinsler

The president's assistant, Samantha Samuels, walked up to the podium in the White House Press Briefing Room. "Ladies and Gentlemen . . ." she announced as she looked out at the TV and newspaper reporters who were gathered there. ". . . The President of the United States!"

The press stood and applauded as the commander in chief strode up to the podium.

"Thank you, thank you," President Martinez began with a confident grin. "Thank you, Miss Samuels. Members of the press. I'll be happy to answer your—" *Cough! Cough!*

As the president coughed, the members of the press raised their hands and shouted to be called upon.

". . . Questions," President Martinez managed to say. "Excuse me. I seem to have a little—" *Cough! Cough!* He was hit with another round of coughing. ". . . Tickle in my throat." The president wheezed.

In the White House kitchen, a few floors away, Cory Baxter watched the president on live TV. Cory was hanging with his dad, Victor, who had been hired as the White House chef not too long ago.

President Martinez had become a big fan of Mr. Baxter's cooking while on the campaign trail. Shortly after his inauguration as president, he'd offered Cory's dad a job. Cory and Mr. Baxter had moved into the White House recently. It was just the two of them, since Cory's sister, Raven, was away at college and Mrs. Baxter was in London studying law.

Cory shook his head at the president's coughing fit. Somebody should give that man a cough drop, he thought.

Mr. Baxter saw the expression on Cory's face. "The President's fighting a cold," he explained. Mr. Baxter carried a pot of freshly brewed tea to the kitchen table. He poured some tea into a porcelain cup on a silver tray.

"Cory, look," Mr. Baxter continued. "I need you to run this special throat-soothing tea up to the Press Room right away."

"Cool!" Cory jumped to his feet. Ever since they'd moved into the White House, he'd been waiting for a chance like this. "I've just got to change."

"Change?" asked Mr. Baxter, confused. Cory looked fine—he wore khakis, sneakers, and a T-shirt. "Son, what do you have to change for?"

"Just want to look good!" Cory shouted as he ran out of the large kitchen and into the Baxter's suite next door. He was back in record time.

"I'm on my way!" Cory said eagerly as he picked up the silver tray.

Mr. Baxter checked out his son's outfit. Cory now wore a dark suit, an avocado green button-down shirt, and shiny leather loafers.

"You *do* look good," said Mr. Baxter, impressed.

"Thank you, Dad!" Cory grinned. "It's my opportunity suit."

"Opportunity suit," Mr. Baxter repeated. He liked the sound of it so much that he said it again. "Opportunity suit!"

Cory rushed out of the room.

"Opportunity suit," Mr. Baxter said to himself. Then he looked at the TV screen. He suddenly remembered that the press conference was broadcasting live to the entire nation. "Uh-oh."

Cory couldn't wait to get into that room full of reporters and television cameras. But he had forgotten just how enormous the White House was.

After hurrying up the kitchen stairs, he made his way down a few carpeted hallways. Finally, he approached a polished wooden door.

A secret service agent wearing a dark suit and sunglasses stood at the entrance. The agent folded his arms and frowned at Cory.

After explaining to the agent that the tea was for the president, Cory was allowed to pass.

Cory walked into the Press Room. *Whoa*, he thought, it's a full house!

Every chair was filled by a reporter or photographer, and every camera was focused on President Martinez.

"Man," Cory said to himself, "talk about pressure."

"*Psssssst!*" Someone tried to get Cory's attention.

Cory looked around and saw the president's assistant, Miss Samuels.

Cory realized she wanted him to stand next to her until she told him to bring the tea to President Martinez.

Meanwhile, the president's cough was getting worse.

"So, to answer your question," said President Martinez, "I . . ." *Cough, cough!* "Maybe . . ." *Cough, cough!* "Are there any *other* questions?" he asked, slightly exasperated.

A tall, slender reporter in a green suit waved her hand.

"Uh-oh," Miss Samuels said to herself. "Don't call on Michelle. Don't call on Michelle," she repeated softly.

Cory could tell that Miss Samuels didn't like this reporter one bit. But the president's assistant was out of luck. The commander in chief smiled and pointed at the newswoman. "Yes, Michelle!"

"Ah, phooey," Miss Samuels muttered.

Cory shook his head.

The reporter stood up. "Mr. President, Michelle Wallace, Intense News," she began. "What can you tell us about that nasty cough?"

"Oh, well . . ." President Martinez waved off the question. "It's really more of a tickle." He fixed his tie and smiled politely.

"Are you sure it's not an allergic reaction to, say . . ." The reporter raised her notebook and pencil. ". . . A sting from a killer bee?"

Miss Samuels watched the exchange with growing horror. She could see what was coming.

"What?" The president paused, confused.

"So you're *not* denying that we're *not* in danger from an attack of killer bees?" Michelle continued, clearly trying to get a scoop.

"No . . .Yes . . ." President Martinez looked bewildered. "What *are* you asking, anyway?"

The reporter smirked and scribbled in her notebook. The president opened his mouth to straighten her out, but he began to cough again.

President Martinez looked around the room. "Ah, Cory!" he said with relief.

Cory questioningly pointed at the cup of tea on his tray.

President Martinez waved him forward. "Yeah, son, it's all right," he said. "You can bring it up here."

Everyone in the room turned to look at Cory.

"Yo, I'm on!" Cory said to himself. He took the cup in one hand, and handed the silver tray to Miss Samuels. "Could you hold this for me, please?" he asked politely. He had to look good making his entrance.

Cory walked up to the podium and handed the cup to the president.

"Thank you, Cory," said President Martinez.

"Uh-huh." Cory had thought he'd enjoy being

on TV, but now he couldn't wait to get back to the sidelines—fast!

The president turned away from the microphone to sip his tea. Cory was about to walk away when Michelle raised her hand.

"Question!" she called out. She waved the pencil in her hand at Cory.

Cory hesitated, and the reporter jumped in.

"Who are *you*?" she asked, looking Cory up and down.

"Me?" Cory paused. Then he realized this was just the opportunity he had been waiting for. All of a sudden, he stopped being nervous. He moved closer to the microphone.

"Cory Baxter, White House resident and American businessman," he smoothly announced. The press watched him silently. At the back of the room, Miss Samuels motioned to Cory to stop.

Not a chance, he thought. I'm just getting warmed up.

"I'm a Scorpio," Cory continued. "My passions are sushi and jazz. And I happen to be launching a line of presidential bobble heads!"

Cory opened his suit jacket.

"Bing!" he cried. He pointed to the Cory Baxter Enterprises logo sewn onto one side of his jacket lining.

Miss Samuels looked horrified.

"Bam!" Cory yelled. He pointed to the bobble-head doll attached to the lining on the other side of the jacket. The bobble head looked a lot like the president.

"Boom!" President Martinez cried, hip-checking Cory right off the platform!

Cory collected himself and ambled back to the side of the room, trying to play it cool.

The president smiled at the cameras and calmly took control of the press conference. "Next question!" he barked.

Radio Disney

Your music. Your way.

Now, there are five fun ways to listen to Radio Disney!

▶◀1)) *On Your Radio...*
Go to RadioDisney.com to find your station

▶◀2)) *On Your Computer...*
Stream Radio Disney LIVE on RadioDisney.com or on iTunes (Radio Area: Top 40/Pop)

▶◀3)) *On Your TV...*
Via DirectTV's XM music channel

▶◀4)) *On Satellite Radio...*
Go to Channel 115 on XM or Sirius satellite radio

▶◀5)) *On Your Mobile Phone...*
Listen to Sprint Radio (Sprint) and MobiRadio (Cingular)

RadioDisney.com